THE
LITTLE GREY RABBIT
TREASURY

By Alison Uttley
Pictures by Margaret Tempest

CONTENTS

THE SQUIRREL, THE HARE AND THE LITTLE GREY RABBIT

HOW LITTLE GREY RABBIT GOT BACK HER TAIL

THE GREAT ADVENTURE OF HARE

THE STORY OF FUZZYPEG THE HEDGEHOG

TED SMART

This edition first published 1993 for

The Book People
Guardian House, Borough Road
Godalming, Surrey
GU7 2AE

By William Heinemann Ltd
an imprint of Reed Consumer Books Limited
Michelin House, 81 Fulham Road, London SW3 6RB
and Auckland, Melbourne, Singapore and Toronto

ISBN 1 856131378

Text and illustrations copyright ©William Heinemann Ltd
1929, 1930, 1931, 1932

Produced by Mandarin Offset
Printed and bound in China

The Squirrel, the Hare and the Little Grey Rabbit

ALONG TIME AGO THERE LIVED in a little house on the edge of a wood, a Hare, a Squirrel, and a Little Grey Rabbit.

The Hare, who wore a blue coat on weekdays and a red coat on Sundays, was a conceited fellow. The Squirrel, who wore a brown dress on weekdays, and a yellow dress on Sundays, was proud.

But the Little Rabbit, who always wore a dress with white collar and cuffs, was not proud at all.

Every morning when the birds began to twitter she sprang out of her bed in the attic and ran downstairs to the kitchen. She went into the shed for firewood, and lighted the fire. Then, she filled her kettle with clear water from the brook which ran past the door, just beyond the garden.

While the water boiled she swept the floor and dusted the kitchen. She put the three small chairs round the table and spread a blue and white cloth. She made the tea in a brown teapot from daisy-heads which she kept in a canister on the dresser, and then she called the Squirrel and the Hare.

"Squirrel, wake up! Hare, Hare, breakfast is ready."

Downstairs they strolled, rubbing their eyes, and wriggling their ears, but the Little Grey Rabbit was already in the garden, gathering lettuce.

"Good Morning, Grey Rabbit," yawned the Hare. "I declare you have given us lettuce again. Really, my dear, you must think of something new for breakfast."

"Good morning, Grey Rabbit," said the Squirrel. "Where's the milk?"

"It hasn't come yet," she said.

"Tut," exclaimed the Squirrel. "Late again. We must get another milkman."

Just then 'Tap, tap, tap,' sounded on the door.

Little Grey Rabbit ran to open it and there stood the Hedgehog with a pint of milk.

"I nearly didn't get here at all," said he. "Such a dreadful thing has happened! A Weasel has come to live in the wood. They say it isn't safe to be out after dusk."

"Oh dear!" murmured the Grey Rabbit, "You must take care of yourself, even if we *do* go without milk."

"Bless your heart, my pretty dear," he smiled. "You shall have your milk as long as old Hedgehog has some prickles left."

"Well, good-day," he continued, "and take care of yourself, and warn those two grumblers within there," and off he hobbled.

"Whatever have you been talking about all this time?" asked the Squirrel angrily.

"Why was the milkman so late?" demanded the Hare.

Little Grey Rabbit drew her chair close up to them. "He says a Weasel has come to live in the wood near by."

"A Weasel, child?" said the Squirrel. "Pooh! Who's afraid of a Weasel?"

But she shut the window and poked the fire, and kept the poker in her hand whilst she drank her milk.

'Tap, tap, tap,' came on the door.

"Who's that?" asked the Squirrel. Grey Rabbit opened the door a crack.

"It's only Robin Redbreast with the letters," cried she. "Come in, Robin, you quite startled us. Have you heard the news?"

"About the Weasel? Yes. He's a great big fellow with very sharp teeth. *I* shouldn't like to meet him on a dark night. Well, I must be off, I have to warn the birds," and away he flew.

All day the Hare and the Squirrel stayed in the kitchen. The Little Grey Rabbit ran upstairs and made the beds. She swept the floors, dusted and tidied up after the other two. Then she got her basket and started out to do the marketing.

"You might get me a new teazle brush," called the Squirrel. "I must give my tail a good brush, it is quite tangled."

"And get me some young carrots," shouted the Hare. "I am tired of lettuce for breakfast."

Off ran the Little Grey Rabbit, in her clean white collar and cuffs, and her basket on her arm. Over the brook she leapt, and then she went into the wood. She kept a very sharp look-out, and ran so softly that the leaves underfoot scarcely moved, and the grass hardly felt her weight. Once she heard a rustle behind her, but she went steadily on and dared not turn her head. Her heart went pitterpat so loudly she thought it would burst, but it was only a blackbird in the beech leaves.

When she was through the wood she stopped a few minutes to rest and nibble some sweet, short grass. She found the teazle bushes growing in the hedge, among some nettles, and she bit off three prickly heads and put them in her basket.

Then, with a laugh of delight, she ran on till she got to the Farmer's garden. She passed the hole in the wall, for the gate was open, so in she tripped, over the lettuce and under the rhubarb to the carrot bed.

"I wish we could grow carrots at home," she said, as she pulled them up one by one and placed them carefully in her basket.

Swish! Swish! a sack was thrown over her and someone hit wildly at her with a rake.

Little Grey Rabbit ran this way and that, in the dark, holding her breath, as she tried to dodge the blows. One hit the basket and nearly broke it, and hurt her paw, but still she ran. Then she found a gap, and out she darted, dodging in and out of the cabbage leaves, with the Farmer running after, close to her heels.

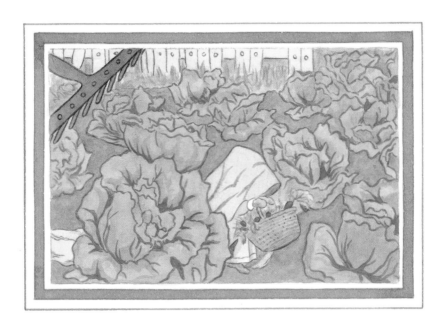

"You little rascal," he called, "you've been after my carrots. Just wait till I catch you." But Little Grey Rabbit did not wait. She could not stop to explain that she thought they were everybody's carrots.

No, she ran for her life, across the field, to the wood.

"I don't think I shall go there again," she said, as she licked her hurt paw, and put a dock-leaf bandage over it. "We must grow our own carrots. I will ask Wise Owl how to do it."

She hurried through the wood as softly as she had come, and reached home safely.

"What a long time you have been," grumbled the Hare. "Did you get my carrots?"

Little Grey Rabbit cooked the dinner, gathered the firewood, and then sat down to dry some herbs and prepare for the next day. She was such a busy little Rabbit she was never still a moment, but the Hare and the Squirrel sat one on each side of the fire and never moved except to put fresh wood on the blaze.

Night fell and they all went to bed, after locking and bolting the door and fastening the shutters.

But when the moon shone in and the stars were twinkling, the Little Grey Rabbit crept downstairs and opened the door. The moon was big in the sky and the stars winked and smiled at her. She stepped out on to the dewy grass, and closed the door softly.

Everywhere was silver white. Leaves and grass sparkled and a thousand sweet scents rose to her little twitching nostrils. How delicious it was!

Although she felt afraid of the Weasel, lurking like a wolf in the wood, she could not help turning head over heels and standing on her head for joy. She felt so young and free!

She jumped the brook three times in her excitement, and then trotted off to the wood. Her feet left a trail of footprints in the grass, so she turned round and walked backwards. Hopping and skipping and turning her head, twisting and twining in and out of the trees she went, with no adventure except a collision with a Pheasant, who rose screaming with fright.

At last she reached the Wise Owl's house, a hollow oak tree. He sat on a bough with shining eyes searching the wood, waiting to start out on his hunt for food.

Little Grey Rabbit quickly waved a white handkerchief for a truce, and he nodded down at her.

"Wise Owl," she began, "will you tell me how to grow carrots like those in the Farmer's garden?"

"What will you give me?" asked the Wise Owl, in a high, crying voice.

"Oh, dear, I haven't anything," she faltered, looking very sad.

"Yes, you have," cried the Owl. "You can give me your tail."

"My tail?" she exclaimed in horror.

"Yes, your tail, or I shall not help you."

"You can have it," she cried bravely, "but be quick."

The Wise Owl hopped down and with one bite of his strong beak he cut it off and wrapped a cobweb round the stump. Then he fastened it on his front door as a door-knocker.

"You can grow carrots," said he solemnly, "with carrot seed."

"Where can I get it?" asked the Grey Rabbit.

"From the shop in the village."

And Wise Owl flapped his wings and flew away.

The Little Grey Rabbit started home again. She stepped into her own footprints, but now and then a shiny round tear fell on the grass, and she gave a sigh.

Suddenly, as she turned a corner, she saw the Weasel standing in her path. His back was turned, he was examining the footprints.

"Ah!" cried he, "a rabbit has gone this way," and he ran along in front of her. Little Grey Rabbit's heart banged and thumped as she followed a long way behind. When he came to the brook he was puzzled, and Grey Rabbit watched. At this side of the water the footprints went to the water's edge, but at the other side, too, they went towards the edge. He scratched his whiskers.

"She must have tumbled in and been drowned," said he, and he went off down the stream, hunting and sniffing.

Grey Rabbit leapt over, ran to the house, upstairs and into bed, where she slept and slept till the birds began to sing.

"That Weasel has been round the house in the night," said the Hedgehog as he delivered the milk next morning.

"Whatever have you done with your tail?" said the Hare, staring at her as she bustled about getting breakfast.

"Grey Rabbit, where *is* your tail?" echoed the Squirrel, frowning at her.

"I gave it to Wise Owl," said Grey Rabbit, blushing and hanging her head.

"Disgraceful," said the Hare.

"Disgracefuller," said the Squirrel, not to be outdone.

A big tear ran down into her tea, and splashed her cuffs. She felt very unhappy, and wished Wise Owl would give her back her tail.

After dinner that day she took her basket and started off on her journey, leaving the two sitting dozing one on each side of the fire. They did not see her go, neither did they see the window open stealthily, and a black nose appear.

Little Grey Rabbit turned in another direction, and did not cross the brook. She went down the lane, overhung with honeysuckle and blackberry bushes.

When she came to the village it was very quiet, for the children were in school and the labourers had gone back to work in the fields. Dogs lay asleep on door-steps, and cats basked in the sun.

No one saw a Little Grey Rabbit with a little grey shadow slip down the road, hesitate a moment outside the village shop, and then run through the open door.

She gazed about her with wide-open eyes. Wonderful things lay all about. Buckets and frying-pans, pots and cheeses, mouse-traps and cherry brandy. She was bewildered as she looked for the seeds.

Would she ever find them? Then she saw the picture of a carrot on a little packet, lying with other packets. Success at last! Here were lettuces and radishes, parsley, and cabbages.

Quickly she seized one of each kind. Then she saw a bag with a yellow bird on it, labelled 'Canary Seed,' so she took that too.

"I will plant that seed and have some little yellow birds as well as carrots in the garden," she thought.

The bag was heavy, and as she dragged it into the basket she made a noise.

Grey Rabbit picked up the basket and fled for the door. She ran down the street as if an army were after her, but all was still, and, except for five ducks waddling across the road, she saw no one.

The journey home was pleasant, and she made plans as she tripped along in and out of the shadows.

I shall dig up that bit of grass under the hedge and pick out the stones. Then I shall sow three rows of carrot seeds. I shall sow radishes next to them, and parsley next. I will dig that good piece in the middle for the bird seed, and when the young yellows come out they will make nests in the hedge."

"Ah," she went on, getting more and more delighted with her plans, "I may get hundreds and hundreds of little birds from this bag of seed, and hundreds of carrots from this packet, and hundreds of radishes from this, and hundreds—"

"Goodness me, whatever is this?"

For she had reached home and the door stood wide open. No one was within. Upstairs she ran, in the bedrooms, in the attic and the box-room. No one was there. In the kitchen the chairs were upset and the table pushed on one side. Bits of red hair from Squirrel's tail lay on the floor, and the sleeve of Hare's coat lay dirty in a corner.

"Oh, my dear Squirrel, my darling Hare," she cried, with tears running down her cheeks. "Has that bad Weasel got you?"

She took a pair of scissors, a rope, and a stick, and started out to look for her companions.

Over the brook she found the trace of the Weasel, and at one side the grass was flattened and flowers were broken as if a heavy object had been dragged along.

"He has put them in a bag and dragged them home," she murmured, as she examined the track. "Poor, poor things! I do hope they are alive. If only I hadn't stopped so long choosing bird seed."

She hurried along the path, which took her through dark and gloomy glades, and brought her to an ugly black house, with the shutters up and nettles and weeds growing in the garden.

Then she lay down under a bush and waited.

A thick black smoke came out of the chimney, and she could hear the crackle of sticks. The door opened and a great savage Weasel stood on the door-sill.

"I shall need more sticks after all," he said. "They will be safe in there."

He shut the door and turned the key in the lock. Then he ran about among the bushes picking up sticks.

"Too-whit, Too-whoo," called an Owl overhead. The Weasel looked up. He was afraid of Wise Owl, and he dared not move. The Owl saw Grey Rabbit, and knew her as the owner of his door-knocker.

But Grey Rabbit made a dash, seized the key, and was in the house whilst the Weasel still gazed up at the foe overhead. Then the Owl flew away, and he wiped his brow.

"That was a near thing," said he. "Now what about some acorn sauce?" And he stopped to pick up a few acorns and carried them in with his wood.

Little Grey Rabbit called, "Hare, Squirrel, where are you? It's me, it's Rabbit."

"Here, here; O, save us, dear Grey Rabbit," cried two piteous voices from a bag under the sofa.

23

Quickly Rabbit cut it open and let the two unhappy ones out, but they were so bruised and weak they could hardly walk.

"Upstairs with you," cried Grey Rabbit, as the Weasel came home. "Take this rope and let yourselves out by the window. I will follow."

Then she seized a stool which stood on the hearth, and crept into the bag.

Grey Rabbit squeaked and moaned, and the Weasel chuckled as he piled the wood on the fire. Grey Rabbit lay watching him through the hole and waiting for a chance. Upstairs Squirrel and Hare fastened the rope to a bed-post and slid down into the nettles. Away they went, struggling through the bushes, over brambles and across ditches.

Weasel opened the oven door. "I'll roast them both together," he said, putting some dripping in the tin. He took a stick and came to the bag. He dragged it out, and raised the stick, and, Bang! Down it came. Grey Rabbit crept inside the stool and lay protected by its legs. Bang! he went on the stool legs, but there was never a sound.

"Dead, both dead," said the Weasel. "Now, is the oven ready?"

He opened the door and took hold of the hot tin. Quickly, Grey Rabbit slipped out, gave him a great push into the tin, and shut the oven door.

Off she ran, not stopping to hear his cries, but running as if he were after her. She never stopped till she got home, and as she sat panting in an arm-chair, the other two limped in.

"Oh, Grey Rabbit," they both said, "we want to tell you we are very sorry for our behaviour. We shall never be proud and rude again. We have had our lesson. You saved us from the Weasel, and if ever he comes here again—"

"He won't, he is roasted by now," she interrupted and told them all her adventures.

"Grey Rabbit," said Squirrel solemnly, shaking her paw for emphasis, "you shall always have the rocking-chair, and sit by the fire. You shall have your breakfast in bed, you shall have toast and coffee."

But Grey Rabbit laughed. "I don't want to lie in bed, I like to work, and I don't want toast and coffee, but I should like to sit in the rocking-chair sometimes, and I should like a party."

So they all lived happily together, and had a fine crop of radishes and carrots, and onions, but no little yellow birds came up.

Sometime I will tell you how Grey Rabbit got her tail back again.

How Little Grey Rabbit
Got Back Her Tail

ONE COLD MARCH MORNING Little Grey Rabbit awoke at dawn, for this was to be a busy day.

Softly she opened her door and listened. Snores could be heard coming from Hare's room, and squeaky little grunts from Squirrel's.

She crept downstairs, took down a round wicker basket and then went out into the raw air.

The sun had not risen, and a star was still in the sky, "like a candle for a little rabbit," she thought.

As she walked down the garden path she looked back at the shut windows, and waved a paw to her sleeping friends in the little house.

She turned down the lane and scampered over the stones, leaping over thorny briars, and swinging her basket round and round over her head.

A startled mouse gazed after her. "I wonder where she is going? It's a pity she's lost her tail, she must feel cold. They say it is fastened up on Wise Owl's door, but may I never see it!"

Grey Rabbit came to an opening in a hedge, and climbed through, tearing her apron on a curved thorn.

She stopped to pin it with a straight pin from a hawthorn bush, and to sip the water from a gurgling spring, like a small fountain in the grass.

Then she ran across the wet meadow to a bank where the first primroses were growing. She put down her basket and began to pick them, biting off their pink stalks, and putting the yellow blossoms in the basket.

When she finished there, she ran to another field, and another, and another, with a basket now heaped with petals. Behind her she left a trail of small footprints which scarcely pressed down the grey-green grass.

Suddenly a black nose and two pink hands with funny little human fingers stuck out of the earth in front of her. She started back.

"Oh! Oh! Moldy Warp, how you frightened me!" she exclaimed, with her paw on her fluttering heart. "Wherever have you come from?"

"I was asleep, Grey Rabbit, but you woke me, so I came out to see who it was," and the Mole shook off the red soil clinging to his bare feet and wiped his hands on the grass.

"What are you doing out here so early, Grey Rabbit?"

"I am picking primroses for Primrose Wine," answered the Rabbit. "Hare has a bad cold and it's a certain cure. My mother used to make it."

"What a clever Rabbit you are!" said the Mole admiringly. "But where is your tail?" he added, blinking his small eyes.

Grey Rabbit told how she gave her tail to Wise Owl in return for his advice on gardening.

"I didn't know Owl was a gardener," said Moldy Warp shortly. "I thought I was the best digger hereabouts."

"Of course you are, Moldy; there is no one like you except Badger. Owl told me about seeds, carrot seed, and lettuce seed."

"Oh! He did, did he?" muttered the Mole; "and he took your tail, did he?"

"No, I gave it to him," returned Grey Rabbit sadly.

"Grey Rabbit," said the Mole solemnly, "would you like your tail back, very very much?"

"Very very much," answered Grey Rabbit mournfully, "but Owl is a kind of friend, and he must not be made my enemy."

"I'll help you, Grey Rabbit," said the Mole, striking his breast with his hand, just as a long level sunray shone across the field and turned his velvet waistcoat red. "I will think out a plan and we will get it back."

"Good-bye, and thank you, Moldy Warp," said the Rabbit. "I must run now, or I shall be late for breakfast," and off she ran with her flowers bobbing up and down in the basket.

At the little house by the Wood, there was dismay when Grey Rabbit was missed. Hare ran up and downstairs with his head in a red cotton handkerchief, calling, "Where are you, Grey Rabbit? A-tishoo! Are you hiding, Grey Rabbit? A-tishoo!"

But the Squirrel saw the basket was gone, and guessed the Rabbit was busy somewhere.

"Help me to get the breakfast, Hare, instead of calling like that," she scolded.

Hare wiped his eyes and sneezed violently. "A-tishoo! A-tishoo!" went he, and he swept the tablecloth off the table and wrapped it round his shoulders.

"Oh, do be careful!" exclaimed Squirrel, indignantly seizing the cloth and shaking it.

She reset the table, made a dish of scrambled ants' eggs, and drew up the chairs.

"Rat-a-tat-tat" came Hedgehog with the milk.

"Late again! Have you seen Grey Rabbit?" asked Squirrel.

Hedgehog shook his old head. "No," said he, "I've been too busy a-milking my cow. She wouldn't lie still this morning, and I had to chase her all over the field. Is Little Grey Rabbit missing?"

"Of course she is or I should not ask you," snapped the Squirrel.

"Sorry, no offence," said the Hedgehog, picking up his milkcan. "I can't abide that pair," he muttered. "Now, Little Grey Rabbit is a nice little thing."

A light footstep came up the lane and a voice was heard singing:

"Primroses, Primroses,
Primroses fine,
Pick them and press them,
And make yellow wine."

The Grey Rabbit tripped up to him. "Good-morning, Hedgehog. Have you brought the milk?"

"Yes, and had my head snapped off by those two. They think another Weasel has you," and he laughed grimly.

She opened the gate and ran to the house.

"Hare! Squirrel! Look at my primroses, a basketful, picked with the dew on them, to make Primrose Wine and cure your cold, Hare!"

All day they made the wine. Grey Rabbit packed the heads in layers in a wooden cask, tightly, and between each layer she put an acorn-cup of honey and a squeeze of wood-sorrel juice.

Squirrel filled the kettle many times from the brook, and put it on the fire. Grey Rabbit poured the boiling water over the flowers until the cask was full. Then she sealed it with melted bees-wax and buried it in the garden.

"How tired I am," said Hare as they sat down to tea.

"How tired I am," said Squirrel.

"How glad I am the wine is made," said Grey Rabbit, as she poured out the tea and cut the bread and carrot.

"When can we have some?" asked Hare.

"In twenty-four hours," said the Rabbit, and Hare began to count the minutes, and to sneeze very loudly.

That night Wise Owl flew over the house.

"Too-Whit, A-Tishoo! Too-whoo, A-tishoo!" he cried. "Too-Wishoo-oo-oo! Too-Whoosh-oo-oo!"

As he flew far over fields and woods there came a faint Tishoo-oo-oo floating in the wind.

"Poor Wise Owl," murmured Grey Rabbit to her blanket, "I must take him a bottle of Primrose Wine, too."

The next day Squirrel, dressed in a brown overall, worked in the garden, digging the soil, and sowing fresh dandelion and lettuce seed.

Hare sat sneezing by the fire, playing noughts and crosses against himself. He always won, so he was happy.

Grey Rabbit had something to do. She sat in the rocking-chair mending her torn apron. Her needle ran in and out, and the tiny bobbins of cotton emptied themselves as she sewed.

At last she finished and put away her work. Squirrel came in, stamping her feet and crying out against the cold.

"It's bitter to-day, Grey Rabbit. Where's my teazle brush? It's time you got me another."

Grey Rabbit found the brush in the wood-scuttle, where Squirrel had thrown it.

She brushed and combed the Squirrel's tail until it was glossy and bright again.

After dinner she left Hare explaining how to win at noughts and crosses to Squirrel, who could never understand, and away she went over the brook and through the Wood with her basket.

The trees were bare, but here and there a honeysuckle waved tender green leaves as it climbed up a nut-tree.

The Rabbit stopped to look longingly at a horse-chestnut whose sticky buds were beyond her reach.

"If only Squirrel would come in the Wood again," said she, "we could have such delicious meals!"

It was very quiet; no rabbits ran among the undergrowth, no birds sang in the tree-tops, only now and then a rook flew overhead, or a pheasant scattered the beech-leaves which covered the ground. The Rabbit's heart thumped, she was always nervous in this Wood. Her ears were pressed back and her eyes looked all ways at once, but nothing came to alarm her.

At last she ran through the gate and entered the Teazle-field. She bit off a few heads, all dry and prickly, and then she filled her basket with curling shoots of young green bracken, which she found hidden under the dead-gold fronds.

Home she ran, softly through the Wood, stepping on the soft moss and mould, and avoiding the rustling leaves.

"Robin Redbreast has been with a letter for you," said Squirrel, emptying the basket in the larder and putting the brushes in a cupboard.

Grey Rabbit took the tightly-sealed leaf-envelope, and broke open the brown flap.

"Who is it from?" asked the curious Hare.

"It's Moldy Warp's writing," answered Rabbit, as she turned the letter up and down, inside and out.

"What does it say?" asked Squirrel.

"It says 'Found Knock Mole,'" said Rabbit.

"Whatever can it mean?" they all asked.

Hare said, "Moldy Warp has been found knocked over."

Squirrel said, "Mr Knock has found Mole."

Grey Rabbit said, "Mole has found a Knock, but who has lost one?"

As the evening wore on Hare got more and more excited, until he could hardly bear to wait for Rabbit to dig up the cask.

The seals were broken and such a delicious smell came into the room, like pine forests, and honeysuckle, and limetrees in flower.

Grey Rabbit filled a bottle and tucked it under her arm. "I'm going off at once with this bottle to Wise Owl," said she.

It was a dark night, and the Wood was full of little sounds, rustles and murmurs. Grey Rabbit felt very frightened, for they were not comfortable homely sounds, and she looked up at the blinking stars.

"A-tishoo! A-tishoo! Tishoo!" came echoing through the trees, and she caught sight of Owl's shining eyes, and her own little white tail hanging on the door of the oak tree.

"Wise Owl, I've brought you some Primrose Wine for your sneeze," said she.

"Thank you, Grey Rabbit, thank you kindly. Even old Owl could not make Primrose Wine. What would you like, Grey Rabbit?"

She hesitated and looked at her forlorn tail.

"No, Grey Rabbit, I could not part with that, unless you bring me a bell to go Ting-a-ling-a-ling when visitors call. But here is a book of riddles."

"But, Wise Owl, where shall I find a bell?" said poor Grey Rabbit who sadly wanted her tail.

Grey Rabbit ran home again with the book in her paw, but her thoughts full of the bell.

Squirrel and Hare were sitting up for her, and between them, sipping from a tea-cup, sat the Mole.

"Here she comes! Here she comes!" they cried, as the latch rattled and she flung open the door.

"Mole has something for you," said Hare excitedly.

Mole brought out a large silver penny, with an eagle on one side and an emperor on the other.

"It's Roman," he said. "I thought it would do for Wise Owl's door-knocker."

"Oh, you kind Moldy Warp! Do you mean instead of my tail? Alas! Wise Owl will only give it to me for a bell."

"A bell? Where can we get a bell?"

"A bell rings people to Church," said Hare.

"There is a bell in the village shop," said Grey Rabbit.

"A bell calls the children to school," said Squirrel.

"There are Hare-bells, Blue-bells and Canterbury-bells," said Hare.

"I might make a bell," said the Mole, holding the penny in his strong hands. "I will bend it and bend it and twist it with my fingers till—"

And he walked musingly out of the house.

"Good Night, Good Night," everyone called after him, but he only said, "And bend it and twist it and bend it," as he went slowly down the garden path with the moonlight on his silver penny.

Hare took the book of riddles to bed with him, and prepared to astonish Squirrel with a joke.

But when he awoke without his A-tishoo, he felt so grateful to Grey Rabbit that he got up early, and went out into the fields to look for bells.

When Grey Rabbit had filled the little blue-rimmed mugs with milk, she called Hare:

"Hare, Hare, come to breakfast."

Hare came scampering in.

"I'm going to the village shop to get that bell," announced Squirrel.

"Oh, Squirrel!" exclaimed Grey Rabbit, "please don't. The old woman might catch you."

After dinner, when the old woman had her nap, Squirrel started off. She put on her best yellow dress, and her little blue shoes, and she tied her tail with a bow of blue ribbon.

She ran with a hop and a skip down the lane, leaping over budding brambles. She entered the village, and found all quiet. She ran swiftly across the empty market-place to the shop, but the door was shut, so she hid in a garden.

Presently a woman came out of a cottage and pushed open the shop door. Tinkle, Tinkle, went the bell.

"It's still there!" said Squirrel.

"A pound of candles, please, Mrs Bunting," said the woman.

As Mrs Bunting reached for the candles the Squirrel leapt at the bell, and tugged and bit and pushed.

The two women shrieked as the jangling bell banged violently backwards and forwards with a yellow animal swinging on it, and they both ran screaming to the Blacksmith next door.

Squirrel kicked her shoes off and lost her blue bow, but she forced the bell, and fell with it to the floor, knocking over three buckets, a milkcan, a mouse-trap, and a basket of eggs. Such a din and clatter came from the shop! Squirrel picked up the bell and ran out of the door, jingling-jangling through the market-place.

"There it is, there it is, Mr Blacksmith. That's the creature and it's got my bell," cried Mrs Bunting.

The Blacksmith threw a hammer after Squirrel which hit the bell, making it ring even more.

"My daughters will say it was another rabbit, when they come home," said Mrs Bunting angrily.

"It's my opinion it was a Squirrel, ma'am," said the Blacksmith mildly.

Away went Squirrel dragging the noisy bell with its coil of thick springs twisting round her tail. Such a rattle was never heard, and the dogs and the cats awoke, barking and howling.

She passed the old brown mare, who shied in a fright and nearly upset the farmer out of the cart. She banged and bumped along the road, up the lane, through the garden, and into the house.

Squirrel was a heroine that day.

But when Hare and Grey Rabbit dragged the bell across the Wood to Wise Owl's door, he put out his head with half-shut eyes and hooted.

"Who's waking up all the Wood? How can I catch any dinner with that hullabaloo? How can I sleep with that Jingle-jangle? Take it away!" And he banged his door, so that the little white tail shook.

They left the bell to rust in the Wood, and ages afterwards it was found by a gamekeeper, who returned it to Mrs Bunting.

When the dejected Hare and Grey Rabbit got home they found Mole talking to Squirrel. He had brought a silver bell, a little bigger than a Hare-bell, a little less than a Foxglove-bell, with a tiny clapper of a hawthorn stone, hung on a hair from a white mare's tail.

When he shook it a sweet silvery tinkle came from it, so delicate, so thin, so musical, that Squirrel and Hare looked round to see if a Jenny Wren was in the room, and Grey Rabbit looked out to see if the stars were singing.

All round the bell Moldy Warp had made a pattern of lines like a shell, and in the middle the eagle spread his wings. They hung up the bell by its twist of sheep's wool, and listened to the song of bees and flowers and rippling sunny leaves, and deep moss which it sang to them.

Grey Rabbit started off with it as soon as it was dusk. She felt no fear as she carried it through the Wood, for the Wood held its breath to listen.

"What is that?" asked Wise Owl, as he peered down from his branch.

"A bell for my tail," said Grey Rabbit boldly, and she tinkled the little silver bell.

Owl climbed down. "You shall have your tail, Grey Rabbit. Give me the bell. It is soft," he went on; "It is beautiful, for it is like a flower. It is wise, for it lived in the beginning of the world."

So he hung up the bell on his front door, and there it sang with every breeze. And he gave Grey Rabbit her soft white tail in exchange. He fastened it on with threads of Stitch-wort, and anointed it with the Herb of St John, so that by the time Grey Rabbit reached home again her tail was as good as ever.

But Moldy Warp took with him to his house under the green fields a bottle of Primrose Wine and the thanks of the little company.

The Great Adventure of Hare

I T WAS A LOVELY MIDSUMMER morning, and Hare looked out of his bedroom window on to the fields where cloud shadows were running races. Gentle blue butterflies and fierce little wasps flew among the flowers in the garden below. Hare stroked his whiskers and said, "Just the day for my adventure."

"Grey Rabbit, Grey Rabbit, come here," he called over the banisters, "and bring my walking-stick, will you?"

A scamper of little feet echoed on the brick floor in the kitchen, and Grey Rabbit ran upstairs with a cherrywood stick and a teazle brush. Hare took down his new blue coat from the hook behind the bedroom door. He put it on, with Grey Rabbit's help, twisting his head to get a good view of the two brass buttons at the back. Grey Rabbit brushed off some tiny specks of whitewash with her teazle. She had to stand on tip-toes to reach his shoulders, she was so small.

"Are my buttons all right?" asked Hare.

"Yes, like two looking-glasses," replied Grey Rabbit, as she gave each one a rub with a duster, and then peeped at her face in the dazzling buttons.

"Don't forget your watch," she added, as the Hare started downstairs.

"Oh dear, how careless you are, Grey Rabbit," said the Hare, taking a large flat silver watch from the chest of drawers, and putting it in his waistcoat pocket. "I nearly went without it."

"Good-bye, Squirrel," called Hare, as Squirrel looked up from the mittens she was knitting. "Good-bye, I'm off on my great journey. Good-bye, Grey Rabbit, I shall be back for supper, and mind there is something nice."

He stepped out of the little door into the sunshine.

"Take care of yourself," cried Grey Rabbit, running after him and waving her paw. "Mind the traffic, and give Toad our present."

"Don't forget to bring a present back," called Squirrel.

He was going to visit the famous Toad who lived in the Ash Wood. Squirrel had laughed when he said he was going and said, "You never dare."

"Darsen't I?" he said. "You'll see!"

Grey Rabbit decided to give the house a summer-cleaning whilst he was away. So Squirrel took her knitting up an apple-tree to be out of the way, and Little Grey Rabbit, with scrubbing brush and pail, prepared to clean the rooms.

Hare shut the garden gate with a bang, and prepared to leap over the brook.

But he changed his mind, and sat down by the water, as a mocking voice cried, "Haven't you gone yet? You'll never get to Ash Wood if you don't start," and he saw Squirrel's face peering down from the apple-tree.

Hare marched off pretending not to hear. He entered the big wood where Wise Owl lived and walked warily, fearfully, on the soft moss.

Suddenly he bumped into a scared rabbit, who was looking behind him. Both fell head over heels but the rabbit picked himself up, and ran on.

A sound came from behind a tree, and a Cock Pheasant walked out with proudly lifted legs.

"Good morning, Pheasant," said the Hare. "It's a fine day to-day. I've just had a tumble - some stupid rabbit, not looking where he was going."

"Hush," whispered the Pheasant.

"Why, what's the matter? Don't you live here?" asked Hare.

"No, my home is in the glade yonder," said the Pheasant, "but I don't want these fellows to know. Too many shady people in this wood. Only last week I had my water-butt emptied and my larder ransacked by a thief."

"Who was it, do you think?" asked Hare.

"It was Jay; he left a bit of his blue scarf behind him," and saying this, the Pheasant flew away with a heavy flap of his wings.

Hare ran on until he came to a great oak tree with a little door, and a silver bell hanging by a thin rope.

"Should I ring Moldy Warp's bell?" thought he. "Suppose Owl should come. What could I say? I'll ask the way to Ash Wood."

He pulled the string and "Tinkle, tinkle" sang the tiny bell. Hare got ready to run, but a sleepy voice called, "What do you want, Hare?" and Owl looked out, blinking in the sunlight.

Hare faltered, "Er — er — er — which way is the way to Ash Wood, please, Wise Owl?"

The Owl looked down severely, and Hare quickly got out his silk handkerchief from his coat pocket and waved it violently.

"What do you mean by waking me up for such a question? Where is your money?"

Hare started, remembering how Little Grey Rabbit had lost her tail; but Owl had seen his shining buttons.

"I'll take those buttons from the back of your coat," said he, and he clambered down, and cut them off.

"Go through the wood and the Teazle field, through the village, across the railway line, through Bilberry Wood, past Home Farm, and the Ash Wood is at the top of the hill," said the Owl, all in one breath. "A Fox lives in Bilberry Wood," called Wise Owl.

Hare turned pale. Owl had already climbed upstairs and shut the door.

Overhead a loud screaming laugh startled Hare, who stood undecided and alarmed. A blue Jay, who had been listening, flew by.

"Ha-ha! ha-ha! Frightened Hare! Timid Hare!" he mocked.

Hare grabbed his stick, straightened his shoulders, and began to whistle, "Rule, Britannia" which annoyed the Jay, and off he went.

"I expect the Fox won't notice me. I'm a pretty fast runner," said he.

He ran through the seeding blue-bells, and purple foxgloves flowering under the nut trees and great oaks.

He ran down the stony path, where ants laboured among the patches of yellow pimpernel, under the roof of beech and elm, to the gate at the end of the wood.

In the Teazle field were red butterflies gathering honey from the ragwort, brown bumble bees, eager to talk to anyone, busy hoverflies, with no time to spare, red-caped ladybirds and field mice in bonnets and shawls, running on errands, strolling home, gossiping by the tiny green paths, playing on swings and roundabouts. It was such a busy world after the quiet wood. Hare walked across the field swinging his stick, feeling very important in his bright coat among all these little people.

They all knew Little Grey Rabbit, for she got her teazle brushes here, and Hare answered many kind inquiries about her.

"Where are you going, stranger?" asked a Brown Rabbit.

"To Ash Wood, to visit Toad," answered Hare, pompously.

"My! You are a traveller!" exclaimed the Rabbit, admiringly.

"I am that," said Hare.

"What other countries have you seen?" inquired the Rabbit.

"Well, I've seen too many to tell you about. I'm a very famous Hare."

They pressed closer and stared at him with wide, innocent eyes.

"Will you tell us about Ash Wood and Toad when you come back?"

"That I will, if you meet me at half-past twelve."

"There's a Fox in Bilberry Wood," said a quiet little Hedgehog.

"I'm not afraid of a Fox," cried Hare.

He sat by the spring, put his two paws under his nose, and fell asleep.

He was awakened by the youngest Rabbit who tugged at his watch. Hare sprang up in a hurry; he had slept longer than he intended.

He left the field by a gap in the hedge, and ran along the narrow road through the village.

A tortoiseshell cat arched her back and spat at him, and a dog barked and tugged at his chain. A baby opened his eyes very wide, and pointed at him, and an old man fumbled in his pocket for his spectacles to stare at him.

He leapt the limestone wall and crossed the field to the railway. The gleaming hot rails burnt his toes, and the roar of a distant train terrified him, as he scampered across and hid in the grass at the other side whilst the express rushed by.

"That's a Dragon," said he, mopping his head. "I must be in China. I *shall* have some adventures to talk about when I get home."

He climbed up a steep path into a rocky wood, "on the edge of the world," thought he.

Great cool spaces were about him, and a green roof above, held up by trees like pillars. The softest moss covered the rocks lying about on the ground, and bilberry bushes, jewelled with pink flowers, grew by the path. The sun shone through the lacy boughs and dappled his fur and blue coat with yellow circles. The air was so cold and fresh, like a drink of spring water.

"Can you tell me the time?" asked a silken voice, and Hare saw a fine gentleman in a red coat sitting on a fallen tree.

"Half-past twelve," said Hare, consulting his watch.

"Really? As early as that? Perhaps you would like to see my collection of birds' eggs?"

"Delighted," said Hare, who was flattered by this notice.

"On my return. I am a bit of a collector myself. I collect Noughts and Crosses." And he trotted on, whilst the fine gentleman gazed longingly after him.

There was a curious smell which disturbed Hare. "It must be some foreign scent on his handkerchief," thought Hare.

He picked a branch of honeysuckle and twined it round his head, and held a sprig of marjoram to his nose, but the smell remained until he left the wood and crossed the fields to the stone farm on the high ridge.

Dappled cows stood under the trees, and a score of hens chattered excitedly about the Fox, who, the night before, had tried to open the hen-house door.

In front of him lay Ash Wood. Apple-green moths and honey-bees came to meet him as he entered. The flowers grew in groups, a patch of red campion here, a clump of forget-me-nots there, and tall bell-flowers, in their blues and purples, like mists on the ground.

"Herbs for old Toad, I suppose," said Hare to himself. "He does a lot of doctoring, they say."

In the middle of the wood was a bog, and there, perched on an island, was a small house with a roof thatched with rushes.

"Who's there?" boomed a voice, as Hare waded through the bog with his coat-tails turned up.

"It's Hare, from Grey Rabbit's house, over the valley," said Hare.

The little door opened slowly and an immense Toad waddled out, leaning on a crutch. His eyes were bright as green lamps, and his cheeks were wrinkled with age. He wore a green coat and yellow breeches, old and creased, but Hare felt a shabby nobody when he looked at the wise animal.

"I have brought a present," said Hare, as the Toad gazed at him.

He searched all his pockets, and then took off his coat. He looked in his waistcoat pockets, but it wasn't there.

The Toad stood, whilst Hare turned everything inside out.

"Here it is," he cried at last. "Grey Rabbit stitched it inside my coat-lining."

He cut the stitches and brought out an egg-beater.

"It's to beat eggs, you know, make them frothy," explained Hare.

Toad was entranced. He held it between his knees and turned the handle so that the wheels whizzed.

He whizzed it in a bowl of cream which stood on the door-step. The cream foamed in a whiteness.

"Butter," said he.

"Come in, come in, Hare," he cried, throwing open the little door. Hare walked through to a courtyard, where a fountain played.

Toad beat up the fountain and made rainbows of light.

Then he rang a hare-bell, and two frogs appeared.

"Bring refreshments for this gentleman," he commanded, "and a bowl of wood-pigeons' eggs."

The two frogs returned with saffron cake which Hare ate greedily. The Toad beat up the eggs, and made wonderful drinks which astonished Hare.

"I have no teeth," he explained. "It's a most useful gift, most useful. I have never been so pleased."

He took Hare to a cupboard which was crammed with odds and ends. There were skipping ropes, tin cans and ginger-beer bottles, mouth-organs, matches - all the things that picnickers had left behind.

"Choose a present for yourself, and one for each of your friends," said Toad, and Hare hunted to find something suitable.

He chose a tiny pair of slippers for Little Grey Rabbit, a boxwood flute for Squirrel, and a penknife with a corkscrew for himself.

Then Toad unlocked a secret drawer and took out a small bottle labelled VENOM.

"I shall give you a bottle of my famous Venom," said he, "but take great care of it. You had better give it to Grey Rabbit to put in the medicine cupboard."

Hare put it in his pocket, with the slippers, flute and knife.

As Hare waded through the bog he turned round and saw the Toad busily beating the air with the egg-beater.

It was dusk when he ran across the fields to Bilberry Wood, and a little crescent moon hung in the sky.

"Hello!" said a voice. "You've been a long time," and Hare saw the red-coated gentleman sitting on a stile. At the same moment a strange odour came floating to him, and his heart fluttered and bumped against his side.

"Oh! Sir!" said he, "you quite startled me. I had forgotten about you."

"Why young fellow, I've been expecting you to supper," replied the Fox with a leer.

"I'm afraid it's too late, I'll put off my visit, if you don't mind," said the Hare.

"It's quite early, and really you *must* come, everything is ready," said the Fox.

"I've got a flute," said Hare, "I'll show it to you if you let go my arm."

"Show it to me in the house," replied the Fox, "and then you can play on it."

They arrived at a ruined little house beside a stream. The Fox pushed Hare into the kitchen. Fox was an untidy animal. In a corner lay a gun, a trap, several snares, a jemmy for forcing doors, and a complete burglar's outfit.

Hare sat uneasily on the edge of a stool, and Fox lay back on a broken rocking-chair.

On the table was a very large dish, as big as Hare, a plate, a long cruel knife and sharp fork, and a pot of red-currant jelly.

Hare felt more and more uncomfortable. "I really must go,"

said he, as the stars blinked at him through the broken window, and a little wind moaned round the house. Was Grey Rabbit sitting up for him? Would the Squirrel miss him?

"Not yet, not yet. You've only just come," said the Fox. "Would you mind taking off your coat and weskit? They might fit a young friend of mine."

Hare got more and more alarmed. He handed his lovely blue coat and waistcoat to the Fox, and a paper fell out of the pocket.

"Hello, what's this?" asked the Fox, and opened the paper covered with noughts and crosses.

"It's a game," stammered Hare.

"Let us play," said the Fox, and he drew his chair up to Hare's stool.

Fox learned quickly and beat him every time. Hare was too frightened to look what he was doing; his eyes were glancing round the room to find a way of escape. The door was locked, and the broken window gave the only chance.

"That's enough," said the Fox putting the pencil and paper in his pocket, and he picked up the coat and turned out the pockets. He brought out the silk handkerchief, the ash twigs, a boot-lace, the little slippers, a marble, the flute, and the Venom bottle.

"Hello? What have we here?" said he, examining the small green bottle. "Scent? What? Scent? Conceited Hare to carry scent in your pocket!"

He took out the cork and poured some of the liquid on the silk handkerchief. Then he put it to his nose. His eyes closed, his ears drooped, and he sank with his head on the table, insensible.

Hare sprang up, seized the half-empty bottle of Venom, cut the watch from the Fox's neck with his new knife, swept up the slippers, and the flute in his paw, and made for the window. He scrambled through, without waiting for his coat and stick, for already the Fox's eyes were rolling, and his legs kicking.

Away he ran through the wood, tumbling over stones, pitching into brambles, slipping, sliding, rolling down the slopes, his breath panting, his eyes starting.

At first he had no idea where he was, but a glance at the stars showed him the way. He crossed the railway line, and ran through the edge of the village, where dim lights shone in the windows.

When he arrived at the spring he found four sleepy little rabbits, and a Hedgehog, waiting for him.

"Here he comes, here he comes! Hurrah!" they cried. "What time is it? We've waited for ages."

"Half-past twelve," panted Hare, and he stopped a moment to breathe.

"You've been a very long time," said the Hedgehog.

"I stopped to play noughts and crosses with Mr Fox," said Hare, and they all opened wide their mouths with astonishment. Then he hurried on, up the steep field to the wood.

"It's been wonderful to meet a real explorer," they said.

Hare clasped the bottle of Venom tightly in his paw as he went through the deep wood, ready for any Weasel or Stoat whom he might meet. As he ran out of the trees he saw a candle burning in the window of the little house, and he shouted for joy.

Grey Rabbit and Squirrel heard him, and came running down the garden path.

"Oh, Hare, we thought you were dead, especially as Wise Owl told us there was a Fox in Bilberry Wood," they cried, as they clung to him.

"He caught me," confessed Hare, "and I only escaped through Toad's kind present to us all." He gave a shiver as he thought of the Bilberry Wood and smiling Mr Fox. They entered the house and Hare told his story, and put his presents on the table.

Squirrel tootled on the flute, and Little Grey Rabbit tried on the silver birch slippers, which fitted her as if they had been made for her small feet. The Venom she locked up in the medicine cupboard, among the stores of camomile, wormwood, and rue.

"I've had my great adventure," said Hare. "I am famous all over the world, and now I shall lead a quiet life at the fireside."

He wound up his watch, took his lighted candle, and went slowly upstairs to bed.

Grey Rabbit and Squirrel looked at one another and laughed softly. Then they followed, and soon the only sounds in the house by the wood were the snores of Columbus Hare.

The Story of Fuzzypeg the Hedgehog

EARLY ONE SUMMER MORNING, when the white mist lay over the fields like a soft blanket, old Hedgehog uncurled himself and rolled out of bed.

"Don't wake Fuzzypeg," called Mrs Hedgehog, warningly, as he rubbed his bruised shin, and struggled with a sheet which was all mixed up with his prickles.

Hedgehog managed to get unravelled without spoiling the leaf-linen sheet of which Mrs Hedgehog was so proud. He stooped over Fuzzypeg who lay curled up in bed, a small ball of prickles.

"He'll be a grand fellow when he is grown up," said he to his wife.

Over the head of the bed hung a string of bobbins, a present from Little Grey Rabbit, who lived in the house on the edge of the Wood, and on the floor lay a poppy-head drum.

Hedgehog went downstairs with his prickles lowered, lest they should brush the whitewash off the ceiling, and walked into the kitchen. Mrs Hedgehog polished him up with a duster, and gave him a clean brown handkerchief.

He opened the door and took down a small wooden yoke, and slung it across his shoulders with the two chains hanging, one on each side.

On the hooks of these he hung two little wooden pails, and, hitching them up, he started off to get the milk.

"Don't be late," called Mrs Hedgehog. "Breakfast is at six o'clock today. It is Fuzzypeg's birthday."

The mist was so thick he could scarcely see, but he trotted down the beaten path, through the furze gate, as prickly as himself, into the fields.

He walked straight through the meadow, under a five-barred gate, to another field of short pasture grass. A low deep sound of breathing reached him, and out of the whiteness appeared a herd of cows, dozing as they stood waiting for the sunrise.

"Coo-up, Coo-up," called Hedgehog, and a roan-and-white Cow raised her head and watched him unhook his pails and remove the yoke. Hedgehog gave her a nudge; "Lie down," he commanded, and she obediently lay down.

"There's going to be a fine sunrise this morning," said the Cow.

"How do you know?" said Hedgehog.

"By the clouds, like curds and whey," answered the Cow. "When they are like butter, it will be dull," she continued.

And what happens when clouds are like eggs?" asked Hedgehog.

"Then it will rain!" said the Cow.

"Talking of eggs, I shouldn't mind one myself," Hedgehog remarked.

"Plenty in the hen-house," replied the Cow.

Hedgehog milked steadily. The little pails were soon frothing over with milk, so he politely thanked the Cow, and took up his yoke.

Off he walked, with brimming pails, to the house where lived Grey Rabbit and her friends, Hare and Squirrel.

Hedgehog knocked at the door, and Grey Rabbit opened it.

"You are early this morning, Hedgehog," she said.

"Yes, Grey Rabbit, it is my little Fuzzypeg's birthday," replied the Hedgehog.

"How old is he?" asked Grey Rabbit.

"A year — half-grown up," said the Hedgehog.

"Wait a minute, and I will send him a present," said Grey Rabbit. She came running down with a hen's egg.

"It's a Boiled Egg," she said. "Little Fuzzypeg can play ball with it."

Hedgehog thanked her and walked along the lane to Moldy Warp's house. He went to the door and knocked. It opened a crack.

"You are early this morning, Hedgehog," said the Mole.

"It is little Fuzzypeg's birthday today," said the Hedgehog.

"Wait a minute and I will send him a present," said the Mole. He came back with a hen's egg. "It's a Scrambled Egg," said he. "I had to scramble under a haystack and back with it."

"Oh, thank you, kind Moldy Warp, Fuzzypeg *will* be pleased."

The Hedgehog walked across the field, and under a stone wall, to an old black house. He knocked at the door and a Rat answered. Hedgehog felt slightly nervous at Rat's house, and never turned his back, although Rat seemed a friendly fellow.

"Here's the milk," said Hedgehog, quickly.

"You're in a hurry," said the Rat.

"Yes, it's my Fuzzypeg's birthday."

"And how old is he?" asked the Rat.

"A year," said Hedgehog, feeling uneasy.

"I will send him a present," said the Rat. He ran to his cupboard and took out an egg. "It's a Poached Egg," he said solemnly. "I poached it last night from the hen-house."

Hedgehog put it in his bag with the other eggs. "Thank you, Rat," he said.

There was one more house to visit, and that was Red Squirrel's. Hedgehog knocked at the door, and Red Squirrel came tumbling downstairs.

"You are early with the milk, Hedgehog," said he.

"Yes," said the Hedgehog. "It is little Fuzzypeg's birthday and I must be quick. He is a year old to-day."

"Your little Fuzzypeg's birthday? I must send him a present," and he ran to the top of the tree. He came down carrying an egg, a dark-brown egg.

"It's an Old-Laid Egg," said he, "the same age as Fuzzypeg."

So Hedgehog put the Old-Laid Egg with the others and hurried home.

"How kind everyone is!" he thought.

Fuzzypeg was sitting on a little chair, waiting for his bread and milk, when Hedgehog arrived.

"All these presents are for Fuzzypeg," said he.

Fuzzypeg had the Scrambled Egg for breakfast, and divided the Poached Egg between father and mother. The Old-Laid Egg and the Boiled Egg he kept for toys.

After breakfast, Hedgehog went out with his son to play "Rolling". They climbed up a hill with the eggs, and rolled down to the bottom.

"Bumpitty Bump!" went Fuzzypeg.

"Bumpitty Bump!" went the Boiled Egg. "Squishitty Squash!" went the Old-Laid Egg.

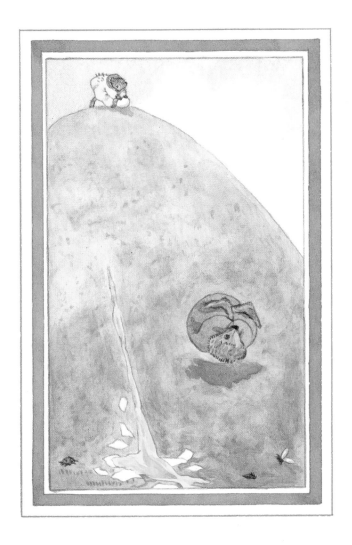

Such a smell arose! Hedgehog and Fuzzypeg took to their heels and ran all the way home.

When evening came and the sun went down in a sea of gold, Hedgehog gave Fuzzypeg his present - a green parcel.

Fuzzypeg opened it with trembling paws. Inside was a little white cage, made of the pith of rushes. Two small black creatures lay within.

As he held the cage, twilight came, and the little creatures sent out a beautiful soft light, so that the cage was like a fairy lantern.

"What are they?" asked Fuzzypeg.

"Glow-worms," replied Hedgehog. "Two tame glow-worms. Feed them and treat them kindly, and then you can let them loose in the hedge-garden."

Fuzzypeg hung up the cage from a hook in the ceiling, and the room was filled with the delicate light. But when he came down the next day, the glow-worms were fast asleep, and so they remained till evening.

Hedgehog was very fond of eggs, and began to poach, but usually he found nothing, for Rat had been there first.

Then, on a lovely September day, he had a great adventure. He was strolling through the fields, holding Fuzzypeg's hand, when suddenly the hens began to cry and hiss and scream.

"Help! Help! Help! Save us! Run for your life!" they cried as they rushed to the shelter of the farm.

All except a Speckledy Hen, who was too frightened to move. She stood staring at an adder, which glided nearer and nearer.

Fuzzypeg trembled and stayed very still, but Hedgehog sprang at the adder's tail, and held it with teeth and hands.

Over and over again the adder tried to bite Hedgehog, but Old Hedgehog never let go until the adder lay dead.

The Speckledy Hen said, shaking, "Hedgehog, you saved my life."

"It's nothing. Pray don't mention it," said Hedgehog, modestly. "It's months since I tasted Hadder Pie. My wife will be glad of this," and he slung the adder across his back, and went home with the admiring Fuzzypeg.

After a fine dinner of Adder Pie, Fuzzypeg ran out to play with his cousins, Tim and Bill Hedgehog.

"I say!" said he, "My father killed a Nadder! He pounced on it and held its tail till it was dead."

"That's nothing," said Bill Hedgehog, scornfully. "My father pounced on a Lion's tail and held it till it was dead!"

Fuzzypeg ran in and out of the slender trees, pretending to enjoy himself, but his heart was heavy. "I don't want to play to-day," he said, and he walked home to his father and his mother through the bracken.

"Mother," said he, "if my father met a Lion, could he pounce on its tail and hold tight till it was dead?"

"Of course he could," replied Mrs Hedgehog, looking up from her sewing, and old Hedgehog proudly rattled the milk pail, and wisely said nothing.

"He could fight an elephant, I expect," said Fuzzypeg to himself. "Tell me the tale of how Grey Rabbit killed the Weasel," he implored his mother.

He made up his mind to be very brave like his father and Grey Rabbit.

Every morning the grateful Speckledy Hen laid an egg under the Sycamore tree, and every day Mrs Hedgehog divided it neatly into three parts, for Hedgehog, Fuzzypeg and herself. She wanted to repay the kindness of the Hen, so one day she made a hay-seed cake.

"Take this to the Speckledy Hen," she said to Fuzzypeg. "Do not dawdle on the way home. Walk on the little green path under the hedge-row, not on the broad white road across the fields. There are dangers about — Weasels, Stoats, Snakes, and worse."

"What shall I do if I meet danger?" asked Fuzzypeg.
"Roll up in a ball, and keep your face hidden."
"Suppose I meet a lion?"
His mother laughed, "You won't meet a Lion," said she.
He trotted through the fields, picking a few mushrooms and blackberries. He sniffed at the honeysuckle, far above his head, and admired the red rose-hips. When he got to the Low Meadow he met the Speckledy Hen.
"Mother sent you a hay-seed cake," said he, "and thanks you for the eggs."

"How deliciously sweet it smells!" said the Hen. "Now come with me and I will show you where the finest acorns fall."

She took him to an old oak tree, and he picked up the young acorns.

By the time he started home it was getting late. The blackbirds were calling, "Hurry up, hurry up," to their children, and the thrush was practising her music for next day's wood-concert.

"Stop and play a minute," said Hare.

Fuzzypeg stopped a minute, and a minute more, whilst the Hare tried to explain noughts and crosses to him.

"'Ware Stoat! 'Ware Stoat!" cawed a rook, as he turned again for home. He would go along the white path, he decided.

He hurried along the broad road, thinking of his supper. Suddenly he saw a great, white, curly-haired animal.

He hesitated, and the animal saw him. It roared, and sprang towards him with frightful springs.

"A Lion," thought poor Fuzzypeg, and he curled himself up in a ball and kicked off his shoes.

The Lion bounced into him, and got a bunch of prickles in his nose.

"Bow-Wow! Bow-Wow! Ow! Ow!! Ow!!!" roared the Lion, and he turned and ran to — Oh! Horrors! Fuzzypeg saw a great Elephant advancing.

"Good Dog, Spot; keep off him!" cried a voice.

"Look what Spot and I found, Daddy! A young Hedgehog!"

"Put it in the garden, Tommy; it will catch slugs."

"No, I won't, I *won't* catch slugs!" squeaked Fuzzypeg. "Let me go home. My father is a great Hedgehog, and he once killed a Lion."

Tommy took no notice, but carried the Hedgehog to the garden, and put him on the path. Slowly Fuzzypeg uncurled and had a peep. Then he bolted for the gate, but he was not quick enough, for Tommy seized him, and put him under an enormous flower-pot. He brought him a bowl of bread and milk, and left him for the night.

When no little Hedgehog came home, old Hedgehog went out to look for him, along the green lanes and byways. He traced him to the field where he had met the Hare, and on the ground there he found a little paper with O's and X's. Hedgehog could not read it, so he put it in his pocket, and followed the track along the white path. A bundle of acorns tied up in a tiny dirty handkerchief lay there, some mushrooms in a dock-leaf, and a pair of red shoes.

As he examined these, he felt a pair of eyes staring at him, and, turning, he saw the Stoat in the hedge.

Old Hedgehog never knew how he got home to his wife. He was in despair as he showed her the shoes and the pathetic little bundles. But Mrs Hedgehog would not give in.

"You must go this very night to Grey Rabbit's House to ask if they know anything," she said. So Hedgehog set off again, under the golden moon.

He knocked at the door, and Squirrel answered.

"No, we don't want any milk to-night, thank you," said she, shutting the door.

"Please, ma'am, it's my little Fuzzypeg, he's lost."

"Does anyone know where Fuzzypeg Hedgehog is?" she called into the house.

Grey Rabbit came running with a half-knitted sock in her paws, and Hare came with a little green book he was reading.

"I've seen him," said Hare. "We met in the Low Meadow, and we had a little game of noughts and crosses. He will be quite good at it if he practises."

Hedgehog took the paper from his pocket.

"Yes, that's it," said Hare.

"What happened then?" asked Hedgehog.

"He just ran on and on and I ran the other way."

Grey Rabbit then spoke. "I am so sorry, Hedgehog. I advise you to see Wise Owl."

"Wise Owl? Oh no, not Wise Owl!" cried Hedgehog.

"Why not?"

"Because," Hedgehog hesitated, "he might be hungry, you see."

"If you wave a white handkerchief for a truce, you will be safe," said Squirrel.

Little Grey Rabbit tied two white handkerchiefs to his prickles, and he went into the great Wood.

Wise Owl was out hunting when Hedgehog rang the silvery bell on the door of the old oak tree. So he sat down to wait, feeling very small and lonely. High up among the pointed leaves he could see the kindly Moon. He crept closer to the tree, and held his nose against the rough warm bark. It was comforting.

"Too-Whit, Too-Whoo," came nearer and nearer, and Wise Owl, who had heard the bell far away, flew to his house, carrying something which Hedgehog preferred not to see.

"Who are you?" he asked.

"I'm Hedgehog the Milkman, Sir."

"What do you want?"

"Please, Sir, I've lost my little Hedgehog, and Grey Rabbit thought you could find him for me."

The Owl was flattered. "Perhaps I can," he replied, "but I must be paid."

"Anything you like," said Hedgehog.

"Well," said Wise Owl, considering, "I will have a quill for a pen and a can of milk, and a new-laid egg. Bring them tomorrow at dawn, and you shall have news of your son."

Hedgehog thanked him and went home.

Wise Owl flew with wide sweeping wings over the fields looking for little Hedgehog, but nowhere could he see him.

"Stoat, have you seen little Hedgehog?" he asked a shifty-eyed fellow, creeping along the hedges with a club in his hand.

"No, Sir," said Stoat. "I only saw Milkman Hedgehog a moment."

"If you see him, report to me," said Wise Owl, sternly.

"Yes, Sir," said Stoat, touching his slouched hat. "I wish I had seen him," he muttered when Wise Owl had flown away.

"Rat, have you seen little Hedgehog?" the Owl asked a dark poacher, creeping under a wall with a twisty wire in his hand.

"No, Sir. I sent him an egg for his birthday, but I've not seen him."

"Report to me if you do," said Wise Owl.

"Yes, Sir," said the Rat, touching his cap, and hurrying on.

"Yard-dog, have you seen little Hedgehog?" the Owl asked a curly white dog, sitting outside his kennel, singing to the moon.

"Yes," answered the dog, "I've seen him, but I shall tell you nothing about him. I belong to the House, and you belong to the Wood," and the dog proudly shook his chain.

"He must be somewhere near," thought the Owl, so he searched the lawn and pigsty, and the orchard.

A little sound caught his keen ears, as he flew slowly over the garden, a sound of weeping and soft sobbing.

"Mother, Mother, Grey Rabbit, Father, Moldy Warp. Come! Come! Oh! I'm so lonely and lost!"

The sounds came from a large inverted flower-pot, standing firmly in the rhubarb bed. The Owl flew down and looked through the hole in the top.

The sobbing ceased, for little Fuzzypeg was terribly alarmed to see a bright eye instead of the far cluster of stars.

"Is that you, little Hedgehog?" asked the Owl.

"Yes, it's me," said the little creature, trembling.

"Help is coming," said the Owl, and he flew away home, for his work was over.

At dawn came the Hedgehog carrying a can of milk, a goose-quill for a pen, and a new-laid egg. He rang the bell and waved the handkerchiefs. Owl, who was just getting ready for bed, looked through the door.

"Put them down there, Hedgehog. Your son is safe under a flower-pot in the farmer's garden."

Hedgehog thanked him and started home at a run, calling on his way for Little Grey Rabbit, Hare, Squirrel and Moldy Warp.

Mrs Hedgehog ran to the door when she heard the patter of little feet, and she joined them.

They all ran through the fields, Hare and Little Grey Rabbit leading, Squirrel coming next . . .

Hedgehog and Mrs Hedgehog panting after . . .

. . . and Moldy Warp far behind.

They squeezed under the gate (except the fat Hare, who had to climb the wall), and ran across the lettuces and carrots, down the little path between the gooseberry bushes, to the red rhubarb, where stood an enormous plant-pot.

"Are you there, Fuzzypeg?" called old Hedgehog.

"Yes, Father, are you?" answered a small faint voice.

"Yes, we are all here," said Hedgehog; "Squirrel, Hare and Grey Rabbit, and Moldy Warp is on the way."

He turned to the animals. "All push, and over the plant-pot must go."

So they pushed and they pushed, but the plant-pot didn't move.

"Steady, boys! Now! All together! SHOVE!!" called Hedgehog, but still the plant-pot did not move.

A large Rat strolled up.

"What are you doing?" said he.

"Little Hedgehog is under this pot," explained Hedgehog.

"Oh, he's found, is he? But you will never move that thing if Hare pushes one way and you all push the other. Now, heave ho!!!" shouted Rat, but as they all pushed away from him, the plant-pot still did not move.

They stuck their little feet in the ground, and puffed and panted and bumped their shoulders. Little Hedgehog inside shouted, "Push harder! Push harder!"

Then Moldy Warp turned up.

"Not that way," said he, quietly. "If the pot fell over, you would all be squashed. This is the way."

He planted his feet firmly, and with nose and hands dug rapidly into the soil by the flower-pot. Earth flew in a shower, and in a few seconds he disappeared down the tunnel he had made. The animals waited.

Then a tiny snout appeared, and little Hedgehog crawled up the tunnel, to be hugged, prickles and all, by old Hedgehog and his wife. A minute later came Mole, wiping his lips.

"I stopped to finish his bread and milk," he explained. "It was a pity to waste it."

He rammed the soil down in the tunnel, and the happy procession started home.

"Don't forget to tell Wise Owl that I found little Hedgehog," called the Rat.

"Come into the garden and have some refreshments," said Mrs Hedgehog, when they got back.

Hedgehog and Mrs Hedgehog brought egg sandwiches, acorns baked in their skins, rose-hip jam, fresh blackberries and cream, mushrooms on toast, and crab-apple cider.

When the Hare, the Squirrel, and the Little Grey Rabbit went home, they each took a small quill pen, which the grateful Hedgehog had made for them; but Moldy Warp wouldn't have anything. He said digging was more in his line than writing, and he had everything he wanted in his castle under the Ten-Acre field.